SUMMER AT SOMERSBY

A Francesca and Joseph DeLuca
adventure story

Written by
RUSSELL WATE

Illustrated by
REBECCA CRAIG

CRANTHORPE
—MILLNER—
PUBLISHERS

First published by Cranthorpe Millner Publishers (2022)

ISBN 978-1-80378-017-7 (Paperback)

www.cranthorpemillner.com

Cranthorpe Millner Publishers

This book is dedicated to my seven beautiful and precious grandchildren. Jonah and Florence Craig who asked me to write them a story. The book is also for my other grandchildren, Elsbeth and Asher Craig who are their sister and brother, and the twins, Charlotte and Emilia Wate, as well as my youngest granddaughter Clara Wate.

Chapter One

Francesca DeLuca was laughing quietly to herself as she heard her brother Joseph banging about in his bedroom. Francesca had taken a hammer from his bedroom that she had seen him hide in there earlier.

Francesca knew that Joseph and three of his friends intended to build a den in Somersby Woods over the school summer holidays. The school holidays had just started and Francesca was excited about all the wonderful things she planned to do during the long summer.

After Francesca had gone into Joseph's room, she

had taken the hammer, which belonged to their parents, and put it on the kitchen table, knowing that Joseph would see it as soon as he went downstairs.

The house was filled with loud noises as Joseph stomped down the stairs and he shouted, 'Francesca don't touch my things!'

He clearly must have found the hammer!

Francesca laughed very loudly and cheekily replied, 'What things, Joe? I wouldn't touch anything of yours!' Knowing that it was their parents' hammer, she wasn't really lying to her younger brother.

'Well, don't go in my room then. Anyway, come on, it's time to go to our tennis class.'

Francesca put her long dark hair in bunches and put on some blue sports shorts and a blue tee shirt. She ran downstairs and joined him, and they both went off together to the tennis class, that their mum and dad had enrolled

them in, for one morning a week for the whole summer holiday.

Francesca was twelve years old, almost thirteen, and Joseph was eleven and about to join her at Somersby High School in September. Francesca was looking forward to him being there with her. Even though she liked to tease him she was extremely fond of her younger brother. As well as having dark brown hair, Francesca had brown eyes, Joseph, on the other hand, was blonde-haired with blue eyes. Their facial characteristics matched their parents, Joseph looked like their mum, and Francesca - like their dad.

When they got home just before lunchtime, Francesca got her mum, Katherine DeLuca, to put her hair into plaits and then changed into jeans.

Francesca sat at the family's large kitchen table and ate the sandwiches her mum had made. She started laughing again to herself quite loudly which made her mum look around at her quite quizzically. As she ate the peanut butter sandwich, Francesca thought about Joseph, who had gone off to the woods on his bike to meet his friends. That morning, he asked his mum for peanut butter sandwiches and Francesca requested egg sandwiches, which Joseph didn't like. Francesca had switched the sandwiches, taking the peanut butter ones out of Joseph's backpack, just before he headed off to have a picnic with his friends in the woods. Francesca laughed to herself again imagining Joseph biting into his sandwich only to find out it was the egg one, which he wasn't going to like.

After she had finished her lunch, Francesca set off to Somersby ponds to look for dragonflies she thought would be there. She had been given a small camera with a good telephoto lens for Christmas, and she had put it in her backpack to take some photographs of the dragonflies. Francesca decided to use her scooter for her trip to the ponds. She was good on the scooter and could reach incredibly fast speeds, and was thoroughly enjoying scooting along to the ponds in the afternoon sunshine. She was looking forward to taking some great photos of the dragonflies.

Chapter Two

Joseph sped down the road on his bike, heading from his house to Somersby woods. Joseph loved his bike. He had been given the bike as a present by his mum and dad, Katherine, and Dr Alphonso DeLuca for his birthday. One of the reasons why he loved his bike was that it looked just like a motorbike. Joseph was obsessed with motorbikes.

Whenever he mentioned them to his grandparents, they always said 'Joseph, you don't want one of those, they are far too dangerous!' His parents seemed to just ignore him when he talked about motorbikes, thinking he would grow out of the interest. But he wasn't going to.

As he got into the woods, he found cycling a lot harder in the uneven ground, mainly because his backpack was full of tools such as the hammer, a saw, nails and rope. Joseph and three friends planned to build a den in the woods. Joseph had found the ideal spot, deep into the woods, about seventy-five metres off of the main path. Joseph marked the spot to turn off the path with a small piece of the rope so the others could see where they had to go. The den was going to be built around the beautiful giant oak trees and Joseph set about cutting long branches that had fallen from nearby trees in the wood.

He felt a little bit hungry so he had a bite out of the sandwich his mum had made that morning. He was looking forward to the peanut butter as it was his favourite. As soon as he bit into it, he shouted out loud,

'Francesca!'

There was no doubt that his sister had swapped the sandwiches. Joseph vowed to eat all of the sandwich, even though he wasn't keen on the egg, and not to give

Francesca the satisfaction of knowing she had annoyed him.

To his incredible delight, Joseph had been given a mobile phone by his parents last Saturday. They wanted him to have one ready for when he started year seven at Somersby High School in September. Although he knew they could keep tabs on where he was due to an app they had installed on his phone, he didn't care, it was lovely, clever, and very shiny.

Joseph sent a message to his friends on the phone, asking where they were and what time they were coming to meet him in the woods. He also told them about the piece of rope tied to the tree branch to indicate where to come off the main path.

Ravi sent a message straight back, 'On my way boss!'

Ravi was a bit of a comedian. Joseph thought Francesca and Ravi would be well suited. Joseph heard nothing back from the twins.

The twins Samantha (Sam) and Jonathan Price arrived

first, they were extremely excited and were making an incredible amount of noise shouting and hollering. Joseph tried to calm them both down, but not very successfully. The twins were very similar-looking, but Sam had long blonde hair compared to her brother's short blonde haircut.

Ravi (Ravinder) Raina arrived puffing and panting. He was carrying a huge bag that had a large tarpaulin sheet inside. The twins helped him to pull it out of the bag. Joseph looked at it in horror - it was bright yellow. Ravi was the cleverest person he knew, but, also, the one, with the least amount of common sense.

'Ravi, what are you thinking about? This is going to be the roof of our secret den. Let me say that again, our SECRET den! Not sure how you think a bright yellow colour will keep it hidden! Really, Ravi? I despair of you!' Joseph exclaimed loudly and excitedly.

Ravi looked very sheepishly at Joseph, and even his round-rimmed glasses looked even more crooked than usual on his face.

Sam who was always the person to calm the friends down, quickly said,

'We could cover it though with all of these lovely green ferns that are all over the woods, couldn't we? That would surely hide it, wouldn't it?'

Joseph wondered why he hadn't thought of that, it was a perfect idea. The Italian in him made him get excited too quickly sometimes. Before they set to work on the serious business of building the den, they munched into the sweets that the twins had brought with them.

Chapter Three

On arriving at the ponds, Francesca swung the scooter handle over her shoulder in one quick, very smart movement, so she could carry it easily. There were lots of people, in particular families there, at the ponds that afternoon. Francesca was pleased about this, as she felt not enough people, including her friends, had time for nature and places like Somersby ponds.

Placing her scooter and backpack down on the grass beside the bank of the biggest pond, Francesca pulled her camera out of the backpack. The four ponds that made up Somersby ponds were an overflow-type system from the River Lymn, which ran alongside them on the outskirts of Somersby. The ponds were full of orchids and beautiful reeds and you could sometimes see frogs in them.

There were at least two different species of dragonflies whizzing around the side of the pond. Francesca switched on her camera and sat very still on the ground. The dragonflies were darting about very quickly so Francesca kept snapping away equally quickly, on the camera, knowing that she could delete what she didn't want later.

After a while, Francesca took out a wildlife identification book that she had been given by her grandparents (her mother's mum and dad) a few years ago. This book had pictures and descriptions of dragonflies. Checking the images on her camera against the pictures, she saw that there were some great images of the Common Darter, which had a red body, so it must be the male and the Black Darter. Francesca loved the huge eyes, that the dragonflies had on their heads.

While looking through a few more images,

pond, but all the families seemed oblivious to what had happened. Francesca was glad about this.

Francesca picked up her backpack and set off scooting along on her scooter, making some loud squelching noises with her feet, as she went along.

Francesca began to laugh out loud - the sight of her in the very wet pink trainers must have been a very comical one!

Chapter Four

Joseph and the twins worked extremely hard together to collect logs and branches in the woodland to make their den. Ravi worked out how to make his bright yellow tarpaulin into a roof for the den by fixing it in a circle, right around the oak trees, using some rope he had brought with him from home.

There was only one occasion when they had to hide low in the bracken, and it was when a mother and three children went walking along the main path through the woods. They had a big black labrador dog with them, which, at one stage, Joseph was sure it could smell him. He was wishing that he had had a shower after playing tennis that morning, but he was in too much of a rush to get to the woods and, to be honest, he was not a great fan of showers or baths. However, the dog only sniffed about a little bit, albeit very close to where they were hiding. Sam was hissing very loudly to her brother to keep still and quiet as he was constantly fidgeting about. Then the dog went off carrying an extremely large stick, which was nearly the size of a branch. This, the gang thought, was very funny as he waddled off and almost tripping himself over with every step because the branch was too big for him to carry.

As soon as the family and the dog were out of sight, the gang went back to the task of making their den. Joseph said 'We should give both, our gang and the den, a name. What do you think would make a good name, Sam?'

'Why do you always ask Sam? I am much cleverer than her, and I have much better ideas!' her brother Jonathan complained.

This brought about huge bellowing laughter from everyone.

'What? What is the matter with all of you? I do, I really do!' Jonathan insisted.

Ravi suggested, 'How about we call the gang All Stars, and the den - the Milky Way?'

The four of them played football for the Somersby Stars under eleven football team, so this was a good fit.

Jonathan and Sam both said, 'I thought Milky Way was a chocolate bar!'

Joseph knew the answer to this as he had been fascinated with Tim Peake, an English astronaut, who had gone to the International Space Station. So, he replied, 'The Milky Way is the galaxy that we, on Earth, and our solar system are a part of. We can often see it in the sky at night. Great idea, Ravi, let's use those names.'

Ravi really was the cleverest person Joseph knew.

Jonathan said, 'Why name them all after chocolates? Isn't Galaxy also a chocolate bar?' Jonathan, on the other hand, really could be the silliest person Joseph knew.

The All Stars gang ran out of time to do any more work on the den. They managed to cover the yellow tarpaulin with enough ferns so you couldn't see it from the woodland path. It was time to head home and they all set off on their bikes.

They were going to see each other in a couple of days when they were going to play together in the summer five-a-side football tournament. The twins' dad, Police Sergeant Price, was going to be their manager. The den would have to wait until later that week.

As Joseph cycled home on his beloved silver BMX type bike, he thought to himself, 'I don't know if I will either be a spy or a detective, or maybe both when I grow up.' As he sped down the hill towards his house, he did an incredible left-handed turn which sent the gravel on the road surface flying. He thought, 'On the other hand, I am most likely going to be a professional motor racing rider.'

Joseph jumped off his bike as he got into his garden and raised his arms triumphantly in the air as if he had just won a race. He quickly and quite nervously looked around to see if Francesca was watching. Luckily for him, she wasn't watching, if she had been, he would not have heard the end of it, with her inevitably teasing him.

Chapter Five

The next morning, Francesca walked into the kitchen where she saw that her mother was just about to go out to work.

Francesca showed her surprise by screwing up her face at her mother and asked, 'Mum, I thought you weren't at work today because Joseph and I are going to the dentist in Louth?'

'Your Grandma DeLuca is arriving anytime now, she is going to take you, I have to go to work today.'

Katherine DeLuca worked as a physiotherapist three days a week at Lincoln Hospital and was already running late, so she didn't have time for any of

Francesca's silly faces, protests and arguments.

This didn't stop Francesca though who continued by saying, 'Mum, you cannot be serious, have you seen how crazy and fast Grandma drives? You can't do this to me and Joseph. Surely you should be thinking about your children's safety?'

Just as Francesca finished talking, the front door burst open, and into the kitchen walked her grandma. She was a pretty large lady who had short curly brown hair with streaks of grey throughout it, she was not much taller than Francesca, and although she had lived in England for over forty years, she still spoke in a mixture of Italian and English.

'My *bambino*, you are so *bella*! Come on, where is Joseph, we have to go to the dentist!'

Francesca's mum smiled at her sweetly and without saying another word kissed Grandma DeLuca on both cheeks and left the house. Francesca tried desperately to get out of the strong and smothering hug that her grandma had now placed her into. Luckily for her, when Joseph came into the room, she transferred the hugging to him.

Francesca had decided to sit in the front of the car so she could try and supervise her grandma's driving. However, no chance of that as they roared off down the road very jerkily as if there were no gears in the car to be found.

'Grandma, we haven't even got our seat belts on yet. Slow down!'

'What are you two doing? *Rapidamente, rapidamente*, get those seatbelts on!'

They sped off down the road in Grandma's battered old bright blue (well it was, once) Ford Fiesta. Francesca looked across at her grandma who had, luckily, put her glasses on. One problem in Francesca's eyes was that she felt her grandma could only just see over the steering wheel, which worried her greatly.

'Grandma, didn't you see, that we should be giving way there. You can't see where you are going. Can you? Please slow down! Why aren't you changing gear?' Francesca shouted at her as the car engine roared under the strain of being in too low a gear.

Luckily, the journey to Louth was only ten miles and took about twenty minutes. Joseph seemed oblivious to Francesca's constant worrying shouts across at their grandma, who just carried on driving. One thing that did worry both of them, and Francesca in particular, was whenever Grandma went to speak to Francesca, she took her eyes totally off the road and looked squarely at her whilst talking.

This caused even more shouting from Francesca who said, 'Grandma, keep your eyes on the road, stop looking at me when you are talking.' It had the opposite effect as her grandma then looked straight at her to answer.

'My *bambino*, non-worries, everything is *bene*.'

They pulled up outside the dentist. When getting out of the car, Francesca made out that her legs, in fact, her whole body was shaking, due to how scared she was. This made both Joseph and Grandma DeLuca laugh at how silly they thought she was being. This made her shake even more. Francesca was a comedian!

Chapter Six

Joseph and Francesca went into the dentist's surgery and were asked to sit in the waiting area. After a very short while, Francesca was called in first. Joseph, who was starting to feel a bit bored, picked up the local Louth newspaper. As he read it, he saw that there had been a

number of break-ins at various shops in the town last week, one of which was at a sports shop where lots of training shoes had been stolen. Joseph had often gone in here with his mother to buy various items of sports clothing or equipment. Another one was at a jewellery shop and watches had been taken, and there had been one at the hardware store where tools had been stolen.

Joseph wondered what was going on as Louth was normally a very quiet town with little to no crime. He thought he would ask the twins' dad, Sergeant Price, about the break-ins when he saw him at the five-a-side football match tomorrow. It seemed, according to the newspaper report, that the police had no clue as to who had carried out the burglaries other than they had all happened the same way by using a long handed screwdriver on a back door.

Francesca came out pretending that she was in lots of pain holding her jaw with her hand over her mouth. She was shaking her head at Joseph as if to say it is going to be so painful. Joseph never knew whether to believe her or not, so he smiled sweetly and went straight in.

As it turned out neither Joseph nor Francesca needed any work doing and the visit to the dentist had been painless.

Grandma DeLuca was nowhere to be found so they both just waited by the car. It wasn't long before they saw her waddling along the road towards them, her red velvet hat was all lopsided on her head. She had been shopping and was laden down with bags which she placed in the boot of the car.

Joseph decided to sit in the front of the car this time to try and stop Francesca from making such a fuss about Grandma's driving. He immediately put all the windows down in the car and turned the car radio on full blast, and started singing a Queen song, *We Are The Champions*, at the top of his voice, which Grandma joined in as well.

They both sang very loudly. Looking in the rear-view mirror, Joseph saw that Francesca was joining in, even though she kept shouting at times, 'Grandma, close the windows, turn the radio down, you two sound like cats wailing on a night out!'

Grandma would take both her hands off of the

steering wheel and move her hands and arms about whilst singing, and even when talking. This worried Joseph a bit, but not as much as it did Francesca, who shouted, 'Grandma, put your hands on the steering wheel!' which only made her move her hands about even more wildly. She turned around to Francesca to look at her whilst she was talking to her.

Joseph felt that Francesca was making matters worse, so told her to sit quietly and let Grandma drive. He thought it was best to calm the excitable Italians in the car down by turning the radio off and winding the windows of the car up and keeping very still in his seat. This seemed to have worked as they arrived home safely and all in one piece.

Francesca and Joseph made lunch together with Grandma after they got back from the dentist. Francesca and Grandma had made the pasta dough, then moulded it into ravioli parcels filled with mushroom and cheese. Joseph made the tomato, basil, and pine nut sauce. Yes, it was very delicious. Both, Francesca and Joseph, loved cooking with their grandma.

Chapter Seven

'Yum, yum' thought Francesca reflecting on her lunch as she walked down the hill to meet her school friends.

Francesca asked Joseph if he wanted to join her and her friends. They all thought he was very good-looking, but apparently, he had to rest as he had a big football tournament the next day!

'More likely playing on a computer game,' Francesca thought to herself. Grandma was reading the paper, and secretly dozing off in the chair as Francesca left.

Francesca had put her hair into a ponytail, changed

into short jean dungarees with a red t-shirt, red hairband, and her lovely red sandals. Francesca hoped her friends thought that she looked very trendy and cool.

On her way down the hill, she saw two men cycling uphill very slowly. Francesca said to them very politely, 'Excuse me, you should really both be wearing cycle helmets.' Neither of them had them on.

One of them muttered quite angrily, but not that loudly as he was puffing a lot with the effort of peddling uphill. 'Who do you think you are, telling us what to do young lady!'

'I was just suggesting as it would save you from a serious injury if you fell off of your bike,' Francesca exclaimed as the men continued slowly uphill away from her, chuntering to each other.

At the bottom of the hill, Francesca's friends Ruby, Sophie, and Candice were already there. They had two big banners, one said '*Slow down. Save a child,*' the other said '*Kill your speed.*' There had been at least two serious incidents in the last week of the school term where school pupils had nearly been knocked off of their bikes by speeding motorists.

The girls stood at the side of the road on the grass verge at the bottom of the hill, each holding one side of the banner that Ruby had made. They were chanting and shouting at all of the cars as they came down the hill, whether they thought they were speeding or not, 'Kill your speed, not a child!'

The motorists who were going too fast seemed to be the angriest with them and often tooted their horns quite loudly at them. Some of them, mostly the younger men, raised their fists at them.

The girls had been there about twenty minutes when a very large police Range Rover car pulled up onto the grass verge. The girls were unsure what to do, whether to walk off quickly or wait to talk to the policeman who was now getting out of the car. Francesca told them that they must not run away, but stand up for what they believed in. What they were doing was right.

The policeman was Sergeant Price, the twins' dad, looking straight at Francesca he said, 'You're Joe DeLuca's sister, aren't you?'

Francesca was often amazed how so many people knew this, although they looked so alike Joseph was blonde with blue eyes, like their mum, and Francesca was very dark with brown eyes, like their dad.

Francesca said, 'Sergeant Price (she knew who he was as much as he knew her), we are trying to stop people speeding down the hill. They nearly killed two pupils from our school only last week.'

'I understand you feel strongly about this but you are in the wrong place here. It is too late to ask them to slow down at the bottom of a hill, you need to do it at the top before they speed up.'

'We will go to the top of the hill then,' Francesca said.

'We have had a few people complaining about your

antics, so I want you all to go home now. However, what I will do for you, I will write a report asking for a road safety sign at the top of the hill, saying '*Please slow down*.' The Lincolnshire Wolds Road Safety Partnership is keen to prevent accidents.'

Francesca looked at her friends who all seemed, like her, to be pleased with this as a result. It looked like they had done a good thing that afternoon. Francesca and the girls said 'thank you' to Sergeant Price and walked off together to Ruby's house for a drink.

Chapter Eight

As Joseph's mother was going to work at the hospital, she dropped him off early at Somersby High School where the junior five-a-side football tournament was taking place.

He had felt excited overnight and as a result hadn't slept very well due to this excitement. He had put on his football kit, but not his boots, even though he wanted to before he had come down for breakfast, which both Francesca and his mother found amusing.

Joseph found his friends and, also, Thomas and Billy who were the other members of the Somersby

Stars 'B' team. For the first match, they played Horncastle Tigers 'A' team and were soundly beaten 3-0. The Tigers had won the eleven-a-side league earlier that year so it was no surprise that they had won. Joseph felt quite deflated and disappointed as he had such high hopes of them doing well in the tournament.

He sat next to the twins' dad, Sergeant Price, and asked him if he knew anything about the shop break-ins that had taken place in Louth.

Sergeant Price said, 'How do you know about them, Joseph? Well, it looks like two fairly young men carried them out, we have no idea who they are as there was unfortunately very poor CCTV in the areas where the crimes took place.'

'That is a real shame, were there any witnesses, and were the men in a car at all?' Joseph asked.

'No witnesses but we know one was on a black motorbike and the other was in a white van, but due to the poor CCTV we have no number plate for either of them.'

For the next match, Ravi was playing as a striker,

having sat out the first game and when Joseph passed the ball to him early on in the first half, Ravi dribbled with it past a defender and smashed the ball into the back of the net. Jonathan was in goal for their team and had to make a couple of saves, with Joseph and Sam tackling hard to prevent any goals. They ended up winning 1-0. A great result which they were all very pleased with.

The team easily won their third game 2-0 with both, Thomas and Sam, scoring goals. This meant that if they won their fourth and final match, depending on how many goals they scored, they would finish the tournament at least joint third, a position better than the Somersby Stars 'A' team.

The final game was a tight match with neither team giving any room for the other to even try and score a goal. There were only two minutes to go and the teams were locked at 0-0, Joseph was starting to get a sinking feeling that they were not going to win the match. Ravi then dribbled into the goal area but he was clumsily knocked to the ground by a very large boy from the opposing team. Everyone in the Somerby Stars team, including Mr. Price, shouted 'Penalty!' The referee had no hesitation in pointing to the penalty spot.

Ravi wanted to take the penalty but Joseph had picked up the ball and had no intention of letting anyone else take the shot. He placed the ball down and looked at the opposition goalkeeper who seemed much bigger than he had earlier and he seemed to fill up the whole of the small five-a-side goal. This made up Joseph's mind, he stepped back a few paces, shut his eyes for a moment, and then ran as fast as he could and kicked the ball as hard as he could at the goal.

Joseph sank to his knees and put his head into his hands as he saw that the goalkeeper had got an outstretched hand to the ball.

However, the next thing he knew was when all of his teammates were jumping on him as the power of his shot had carried the ball from the goalkeeper's fingertips into the back of the net. It was a goal! Now with no time left in the match, they finished third. Joseph was ecstatic with his medal and thought that he might wear it when he went to sleep that night! He kept singing to himself the Queen song *We Are The Champions*, over and over again, at the same time smiling extremely widely.

Chapter Nine

That afternoon, Francesca went into her dad Alphonso's study, where he had two extremely large computer screens. Both of these screens were switched on and Francesca saw enormous images of two hands on the screens.

'Dad, what are you going to do with those two hands?' Francesca asked. Dr Alphonso DeLuca was one of the leading hand surgeons in England, although in Francesca's view, the whole world.

'I am going to operate on them tomorrow and replace three joints on each hand as they have all become twisted and they are causing the woman, whose hands they are, extreme pain.'

Francesca was in total awe of what her dad was able to do as a surgeon.

'Dad, I am really sorry to disturb you but I wonder if I can put my camera card into your computer, please? I have taken a picture of what looks like froth with dots going through from the river Lymn, where it meets and spills into Somersby ponds. I have tried to see what they are but just can't make them out.'

'Absolutely,' her dad said, who took the camera card and inserted it into his computer. 'Wow! Francesca, these photographs you have taken are brilliant!' Francesca started to blush red and felt a real pride in what her father had just told her. He then printed off the photograph of the damselfly. 'Show that to your mother, she will love it.'

They then both looked closely at the photographs of the white froth, but just couldn't make out what it was. Alphonso said, 'It looks like toothpaste to me. You will have to try and get a sample if you can, I am not sure how, but that would be the only way to try and find out what it is.'

Francesca went into the garage and pulled out an inflatable boat that they used to take on holiday with them to the beach. As it was very deflated Francesca also found a foot pump to try and pump it up.

On hearing Joseph arrive home, Francesca shouted to him, 'Joseph, I need you to help me carry this boat to the ponds!'

'Don't you want to know how we got on at the football tournament? Well, we came third and I have got a medal.' Francesca was thrilled for him, but still needed Joseph's help and she was not taking no for an answer even though he was complaining about how tired he was.

They carried the boat together and all the way to the ponds, Joseph complained saying, 'We look so silly Francesca; everyone is looking at us. What if any of my friends see me. This is so embarrassing!'

Francesca ignored him and when they got to the ponds, they saw the large signs that were there saying '*No Swimming*'. Normally, the children were not rule-breakers but Francesca thought 'well, I am not technically swimming.' After Joseph had pumped some more air into the boat, Francesca set off to the area where the white froth was, which looked even larger than it had been when she had last seen it. Francesca got there quite quickly using the oar that came with the boat.

Francesca had not dared to take her camera with her onto the pond in case anything happened and it got wet, so she was unable to take a picture of it, but she was able to scoop a few handfuls into the plastic bag she had in her pocket. Looking at the fluid mixture in the bag didn't help Francesca to know what it was, and when she scooped it up it felt very grainy as well. What she did know though was that it wasn't something that naturally should be in the river or the ponds.

As Francesca paddled back to the bank where Joseph was waiting for her, she felt that the boat was deflating  fast and she could feel her bottom and trouser legs were starting to get wet. Maybe she would end up swimming in the pond after all. Seeing Joseph laughing at her getting wetter and wetter made her paddle even faster until she reached the bank and got out of the boat quickly, telling Joseph he would have to carry the boat back by himself for laughing at her.

Joseph didn't stop laughing as he followed the very wet Francesca as they walked home. This was until he realised that the only way he could carry the boat by himself was to hook it over his head and shoulders, and in doing so he found as he walked along that the dripping boat was making him just as wet as

Francesca.

The two of them must have looked very odd to anyone who saw them walking along, both dripping wet with one of them carrying a very deflated boat on their head!

Chapter Ten

Joseph stayed in bed a bit later than usual the next day. He had felt quite tired physically from the football tournament where he had put in every ounce of effort that he could. It hadn't helped to have to carry the inflatable boat home for Francesca!

The family had had a great meal together the previous evening with both Joseph's mum and dad impressed with his third place in the football tournament. They were also marvelling at the photographs of the damselfly and dragonflies that Francesca had taken. Joseph loved it when they were able to have family meals. He knew it wasn't always possible in other families and was grateful for the chance in his.

Joseph and the All Stars gang were meeting this morning at the den, which was now called the Milky Way, so he made his way to the woods on his bike to be there earlier than the others.

When he arrived at the Milky Way, Joseph went behind the den to the edge of the wood where there was a big oak tree that he thought must be at least one hundred years old. There was a ditch that sometimes was filled with water, but was dry in the summer, that separated the wood from the farmer's field.

Joseph climbed up a few branches of the tree and tied around one of the huge, big branches of the tree, a strong rope that he had brought with him from home. The gang intended to make a rope swing. As Joseph sat on a large branch, he looked across at the wheat field, it wouldn't be long before the combine harvesters would be harvesting the wheat. Joseph saw that the farmer had left quite a large margin around the huge field, this, his sister had told him previously, was for encouraging wildflowers, insects, small mammals, and birds. Joseph had to agree with his sister that it was a wonderful thing to do.

Joseph also saw two large Red Kites flying very gracefully in the sky; he loved their distinctive long reddish-brown forked tails. He was amazed that they had nearly become extinct in England, but he had been seeing them regularly. As he knew his friends would be arriving shortly, Joseph was just about to climb down when he heard the sound of a motorbike.

When he looked across to the housing estate on the edge of the wood, Joseph saw that there was a white van, as well as the motorbike at a lock-up garage right on the edge of the estate next to the wood. The two men who were there, were moving boxes out of the van and into the garage.

For absolutely no reason, Joseph felt that these must be the two men who had committed the shop break-ins in Louth. They were too far away for Joseph to see exactly what they looked like, or the number plates for their vehicles. Suddenly, one of them looked directly at Joseph who almost fell off the branch in his haste to get out of sight and scramble down the tree.

When the others arrived, Joseph told them to put their bikes out of sight behind the den, then they all quickly got inside and sat very quietly, just in case the men came looking for Joseph. They had a bottle of Coke that Joseph brought and the milk chocolate hobnob biscuits Ravi's mum had given to him for them to have a snack.

Joseph told them everything he knew about the break-ins and the men he had just seen. There was no sign of them now, so they proceeded to get more branches in places where there were gaps in the walls of the den. They realised they needed more camouflage as the den was still a bit exposed. After a while, they realised that Jonathan had gone off. Sam said he was being lazy and would give him a hard time when he returned.

After a short time had passed, Jonathan came back. He was out of breath and excitedly said, 'I have got both the van and motorbike's registration numbers.' He had written them down and Joseph quickly made an entry about them on his phone. They were all so impressed with how brave Jonathan had been. Joseph wished he had thought of it and gone to get the numbers. Jonathan assured them that the men hadn't seen him as they were too busy doing something in the garage.

The gang decided not to tell the twins' dad, Sergeant Price, just yet, what they had found out, but they all needed to head home, so set off together on their bikes out of the wood.

Chapter Eleven

After dinner the previous night, Francesca had shown her mum and dad the white grainy froth that she had recovered from the pond.

After examining it in the bag and thinking for a while, her dad Alphonso had a sudden thought, 'I may be wrong, but I think this is a mixture of some form of cleaning fluid, either shower gel or even toothpaste. The grainy feel is possibly grit to get yourself clean.'

Katherine DeLuca after also thinking about it for a moment said, 'They might be microbeads in there as well.'

In response to what her mum had just said,

Francesca exclaimed, 'They can't be, Mum, plastic microbeads are banned in England because they are so dangerous to fish and, of course, the environment.'

The three of them were no further forward, but they all agreed it must have been put into the water further upriver and possibly from one of the factories that bordered the river in Somersby.

The next morning, Francesca dressed in jeans and training shoes, putting on one of Joseph's sports tops. She, also, put her hair up and put one of Joseph's baseball caps on and a pair of her dad's sunglasses. Looking at herself in the mirror, she thought that she looked just like a boy and no one would recognise her. She planned to investigate where the mixture had come from.

The sun was shining brightly as Francesca made her way along the riverbank, she wished she was dressed differently and was wearing shorts and a t-shirt. The first factory she passed was completely closed and boarded up. The next factory was a food produce one. However, the one next to that was a possibility, it was the Somersby Personal Hygiene Products factory.

On reaching the front of the factory Francesca was disappointed with what she saw. There was a security guard dressed in uniform standing by the gates. As she walked by the gates, the security guard, who was an extremely large man, glared at her because he saw her looking around past him and into the factory. Francesca was really not sure what to do as from her initial scoping of the factory she had noticed that there was no way to get in without being seen. She went back to the riverside to see if there was another option.

Examining the fence a bit closer, Francesca was pleased to see that a metal gate to the factory had been left slightly open. Francesca stepped through the gate very quickly and went to investigate, having no idea what she was looking for. Now in the factory as she started to move around she saw that just inside and to the left of the gate were four enormous vats. Francesca looked around but could see no one about, she quickly climbed the steps beside one of them.

The vat was almost full of the frothy mixture and as quickly as she could, Francesca whipped out her camera and took some photographs of the vat and its mixture. She almost fell while placing some of the mixture into a bag that she had brought with her. As she came down the steps feeling very pleased with herself the security guard appeared and shouted at her, 'Oi you, boy, what do you think you are doing in here? I will have you for trespassing!'

Then he ran towards Francesca, who set off towards the gate she had come in by, and with horror, she saw that it was shut. This left her with no alternative but to run back towards, and then dart past, the amazed security guard. As she went to go around him, he for such a large man made quite a quick lunge and almost caught Francesca. Instead, he ended up knocking off the baseball cap. Joseph was going to be furious with her for losing his favourite baseball cap, but Francesca couldn't go back for it, or could she? The security guard was already out of breath and was even more shocked when Francesca ran back towards him running past and swooping down to pick up Joseph's precious baseball cap.

The security guard didn't know which way to turn and was feeling quite dizzy with all the running backwards and forwards, so he decided to just stand still with his hands on his knees and shout, 'Don't you come in here ever again. This is private property, get out!'

Francesca although out of breath herself didn't stop running until she got home. Francesca had managed to do what she set out to do, by finding out, almost certainly, where the frothy mixture in the river had come from.

Chapter Twelve

That evening, Katherine DeLuca was shocked when Joseph announced he was going up to his room to read and have an early night. Alphonso had gone off to the hospital that afternoon to carry out some post and pre-operative consultations with patients. He had taken both of the samples that Francesca had collected, one from the pond and the other from the vat with him, to look at them under one of the strong magnifying lights in an operating theatre to help examine them closely.

Joseph had gone off to his room because he secretly intended to sneak out to have a look around the lock-up garage where he had seen the motorbike and the white van. He just needed his mum to settle down watching one of her programmes on the television. He had borrowed his mum's running head torch in case he needed it, even though it was still a very bright summer's evening.

As soon as Joseph heard the television being switched on, he sprinted downstairs and out of the back door. He had positioned his bike and helmet just outside the gate so as not to make any noise when going through the gate.

He sped off along the road, then down the hill and into the estate. As he got to the bottom of the estate, he stopped and looked around to see if anyone was following or watching him. Joseph imagined and felt like he was a real spy on a mission. When he got to the lock-up garage block, he stopped and peered around the corner, with a whoop of delight he saw that there was no one there.

The garage he wanted to look in was right at the end of the garage block, just next to the edge of Somersby Wood. Joseph took his mum's yellow rubber washing-up gloves out of his pocket and put them on. He had got a new pair out of the cupboard under the sink, he knew he couldn't leave any fingerprints. Joseph tried the door; it was firmly locked; he then went around the side where he knew there was a window.

There were several discarded car tyres lying around the back of the garages. Joseph dragged a few them to below the window and stacked a few of them on top of each other so that he could look into the garage. After he had climbed up on the tyres, he pushed his head onto the window glass to try and see inside. The glass was very dirty and

he really couldn't see through it. Joseph tried the window and was shocked to see that the window was open and he could fit through. Without thinking whether he was making a good choice or not, he climbed through the window and, with a bit of a drop to the floor, jumped down into the garage. Joseph was glad that he had brought his mum's running head torch with him, putting it on over his head, he switched it on and found it illuminated the garage and that he could see well.

The garage was pretty much full of boxes and when he opened them up, he saw that they contained training shoes, watches, and, also, tools. Joseph shouted joyfully - he had been right. Here was all the stolen property from those shop burglaries. He quickly took a number of photographs on his phone.

Joseph felt he was probably pushing his luck to be in there any longer, so went to get out of the window only to find he couldn't reach it, even if he took a running jump, he couldn't quite grab the windowsill. He even tried to stack a few of the boxes together but they kept crumpling and giving way under his weight.

Joseph sat on the floor and felt like crying, he was very near to tears when he thought Francesca could come and help him get out. He quickly sent a message to her hoping she had her phone still switched on. They had a strict rule, phones off by the evening. His phone buzzed and Joseph was delighted to see the message from Francesca saying she was on her way.

In less than ten minutes Francesca arrived, and he had never been so pleased to see his sister as he was now. When she poked her head through the window, not a word was said to tell him off, but in a flash, she lowered down the rope that she had brought from home and Joseph was able to pull himself up and out of the window.

As they cycled home Francesca said, 'What are you up to, Joe? If Mum and Dad had found you had sneaked out, you would have been grounded for the whole summer holiday. I was just going to switch my phone off as well.'

Joseph replied, 'I am sorry, thank you for being such a wonderful sister. The garage is full of stolen property from the shops in Louth.'

'Well done to you, Sherlock Holmes,' Francesca whispered, as they quietly got off their bikes and crept into the house, and up into their bedrooms.

Chapter Thirteen

The next morning as Francesca went towards the kitchen to get some breakfast her dad called out to her from his study.

'Francesca, come and see what I have found out for you.'

When she went into the study, there were two pictures of tiny little plastic beads on the large computer screens. Alphonso said, 'Your mum was 100% right, they are microbeads. Well done Francesca, looks like you have discovered an environmental disaster in the making.'

Alphonso had printed off the pictures that Francesca had taken of the microbeads in the river-pond border and the ones from the vat. He didn't ask, although he had wanted to, how she had got into the factory to collect the mixture. He wasn't going to lecture her about trespassing, as he thought about the good that would come of it, and would outweigh the bad of trespassing. Francesca was a sensible girl who very much knew right from wrong, she knew it was wrong to go on private property.

Francesca went and got her backpack, picked up both of the photographs and mixture that she had collected, and went to leave the house. Her mum Katherine shouted to her, 'Not so fast, Francesca, you are not going out without breakfast.'

Francesca protested, 'Mum, I have not got time, I need to tell someone about what is going on with the river, it is so important.' However, she did sit down and ate the cereal and the toast her mum made for her. Joseph, who it seemed was also heading out in a hurry, was told to do the same thing, both of them eating their food at one hundred miles per hour, whilst their mum shook her head at them but still smiling.

As soon as breakfast was finished, Francesca cycled to the Council Offices for Somersby, which was a boring-looking, red brick building. The receptionist frowned at her, asking who she was there to see. Francesca confidently asked, 'Please can I speak to Natalia Jankowski, the environmental health officer?'

'Have you an appointment? If not, I am sorry you can't see her,' the extremely bossy receptionist barked at Francesca. At that moment, Natalia walked into the building. Francesca looked at her in wonderment, she was just so pretty. Natalia was probably in her late twenties, had long blonde hair, blue eyes, and was wearing a long orange coloured summer dress. Francesca looked at herself wearing her shorts and t-shirt and thought 'why didn't I wear a dress today!'

Natalia said, 'Hello Miss DeLuca, I remember you from our meeting to extend Somersby Wood, earlier this year.' Francesca was so impressed that Natalia remembered her that she was, for once, speechless. The receptionist told Natalia that the girl had come to see her, so with that Natalia took Francesca through to a meeting room.

Firstly, Francesca showed her the photograph of the river and pond, then gingerly picked the river bag containing the mixture out of her backpack. The next picture she showed was her dad's one from the  hospital that had magnified the mixture so you could clearly see thousands of microbeads. Francesca did the same with the ones from the Somersby Personal Hygiene Products factory.

Natalia found herself speechless now, then commented, 'You have made an incredibly important discovery, Miss DeLuca. I need to speak to my manager and someone very important in the National Environment Agency. I am going to cancel everything I had in my diary today to look into this urgently. Please can I keep what you have just shown me?'

Francesca was absolutely loving the positive reaction. She quite happily agreed and gave Natalia her full name, address, and phone number so that she could be contacted for an update.

As she cycled home, Francesca was so pleased with what she had discovered and firmly knew that when she grew up, she wanted to be just like Natalia Jankowski, and be someone protecting the environment. Francesca could not think of another more important job in the whole world!

Chapter Fourteen

After Joseph had finished his breakfast, he was pleased about the fact that he had eaten it quicker than Francesca had hers, he cycled round to the twins' house. Ravi was waiting outside and Sam and Jonathan were looking out from the upstairs windows.

'Where have you been?' Ravi exclaimed, who seemed very nervous and agitated. Joseph had sent a message to Ravi and the twins last night to let them know what he had seen in the lock-up garage and arranged to meet them at the twins' house the next morning.

The door was flung open by Sam who told them to come inside the house. The four of them then went into the back garden to talk to Sergeant Price. He was busy replacing a fence and, on seeing them, stopped to ask what was going on.

Joseph, who they all regarded as the leader of the gang, said, 'You know we spoke about the shop break-ins in Louth at the football tournament? Well, I saw a motorbike and white van at a lock-up garage on the edge of the estate near Somersby Woods. Then Jonathan went and got the numbers of both vehicles.' Sergeant Price swung his head around to look at his son, he didn't know whether to be cross or proud of Jonathan, who produced the piece of paper with the numbers on it and gave it to his dad.

Joseph continued by saying, 'I have been and

checked in the garage and have taken these pictures. The garage is full of stolen goods taken from the shops.' Taking the phone to look at the photographs, Sergeant Price looked cross and said, 'Joe, well, in fact, all of you, should not be putting yourself in danger. I would be very angry with you if it didn't appear that you may have solved some crimes. Let me make a couple of phone calls.'

The All Stars gang didn't say anything to each other just in case it made the twins' dad angrier with them, but they all had quite wide grins on their faces. Sergeant Price came back and said, 'Jim Baxter, who used to be your school's liaison officer, is now a detective in Louth and he has been allocated to investigate these crimes. He asked whether you could get there to see him in an hour. Unfortunately, I can't take you though, could your mum or dad get you all there, Joseph?'

Joseph knew his mum and dad were working at the hospital today, so Grandpa and Grandma DeLuca were keeping an eye on Francesca and him, so he said, 'My Grandpa will take us if we go to my house now.'

The four of them got to Joseph's house but only his grandma was there. It turned out grandpa was playing golf that morning. Grandma said, '*Ciao bambino!*' Looking straight at Sam, she said, 'Joseph, is this your girlfriend? *Bellissima!*'

Both Joseph and Sam said in unison 'No!' Ravi and Jonathan almost fell over in tears laughing.

They all headed off to Louth, Joseph sitting in the front of the car, next to his grandma. He had established a system where he tapped her arm once for her to change gear up, and twice to change gears down. He would grab her arm if he thought she should slow down. It worked incredibly well.

On arrival at the police station, Detective Jim Baxter was waiting for them. He recognised all of them from Somersby Primary School. Jim said, 'I have run checks on the vehicles and they are owned by Tim and Tom Fletcher, they are cousins and we have been interested in them for some time now.'

Joseph showed him the pictures of the possible stolen property in the garage. Jim could hardly contain his smile and joy at what he was seeing and said, 'Brilliant work all of you, and you, in particular, Joseph. I need to take your phone, please.' On seeing the fright on Joseph's face that he was going to lose his beloved phone, Jim quickly added, 'Don't worry, I just need to print off the photographs, it will only take a few minutes, and I will give the phone straight back to you.' Relieved, Joseph handed over the phone. All of the All Stars gang were so pleased with what they had discovered.

Chapter Fifteen

It was seven thirty in the morning when on hearing a knock at the door Katherine DeLuca opened it to see Sergeant Price standing there. He said, 'Nothing to worry about, Mrs. DeLuca, is it okay for Joseph to come out for part of the day with me?' Looking past him, Katherine saw the twins and also Ravinder Raina in the back of his car.

'Is it a football team training day?' Katherine asked, knowing it couldn't be that, as Sergeant Price had his big police Range Rover car with him.

'Something like that,' he replied.

Joseph then hurtled down the stairs and was out of

the door before his mum could say any more comments. So, she just said, 'Be careful, Joseph, and I will see you later.'

When Joseph got into the car, Sergeant Price said, 'Jim Baxter has got the Superintendent to agree to let you four sit in the back of the observation van during the stakeout at the garage. But only if you all remain very quiet. Can you do that?'

The All Stars gang all started talking very excitedly and all at the same time. Sergeant Price said under his breath, 'No, I didn't think so!'

The observation van was more like a motorised mobile home. The four of them looked around in wonderment. One man with a bald head wearing headphones was looking at two screens that were

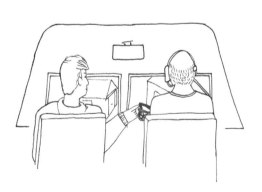 showing two different views of the garage. He told the four of them where to sit,

but didn't seem at all happy about their presence in the van with him. This was until Ravi got out a packet of milk chocolate hobnobs.

'Does Ravi's mum have a never-ending supply of them?' Joseph thought, but was also especially grateful as he had missed his breakfast.

It turned out that being on a stakeout was actually very boring as nothing was happening. Two hours passed, then three. To relieve the boredom, the four of them started touching and pushing each other until the man told them to stop. The police radio occasionally came into life, in particular, when one of the cars watching had gone on a trip and reported that the cousins Tim and Tom Fletcher's vehicles were still at their homes.

Almost another hour passed when suddenly, and without any warning, one of the cars reported he had seen the motorbike go by, heading towards the lock-up garage. The motorbike appeared on the screen stopping outside the garage. The man in the observation van spoke into his radio and said, 'All cars, keep your position; we need him inside the garage and, also, his cousin.'

He looked around and glared at the All Stars gang who were excitedly jumping about. The glare from him was enough to silence them all.

The man on the motorbike had gone into the garage, unfortunately, the cameras couldn't see inside, and there wasn't any audio sound. Then there was a great whooping on the radio to say the white van had, also, gone past and then was seen on both of the screens in the van. The All Stars gang couldn't contain their excitement but this time were not encouraged to keep quiet.

As soon as the man from the white van went into the garage, the radio operator said, 'All cars, get ready.'

Then he said very excitedly, and almost shouting into his radio, 'Strike, Strike, Strike!'

On the screen, they could see two police cars screeching into the garage area then come to a halt which they then positioned their cars to block the entrance. At least five police officers jumped out and went into the garage. Joseph, although he couldn't see it, pictured a fight taking place and the Fletcher cousins being wrestled to the floor and handcuffed. He was right about the handcuffing as they both came out of the garage in handcuffs but it didn't look like a fight had actually taken place. All of the police officers and the four All Stars gang had huge, big wide smiles on their faces.

A very short time later, Sergeant Price arrived to take them home and he said, 'The police operation has been an incredible success. The men were captured and arrested; they are going to admit what they have done. Lots of stolen property is being recovered at the moment and it is all down to you four. The Superintendent says, 'Well done to all of you and Joseph, in particular. You are not just All Stars but Superstars.'

Joseph wanted to sing *We Are The Champions* again but didn't and instead just hummed it to himself in his head, because in his view the All Stars were as the song said the champions of the world!

Chapter Sixteen

No sooner than Joseph had walked through the door in a very excited state complaining that he was starving hungry, there was a knock at the door. Katherine opened the door to see, the lovely Polish council environmental officer. Natalia said, 'Mrs. DeLuca, please could I borrow Francesca for the afternoon?'

'Gosh, my children are in demand today,' Katherine thought to herself.

'Yes, of course, I presume it is to do with the microbeads in the river?' Katherine replied.

'Yes, it is. Your daughter is a wonderful example of

what a young person should be,' Natalia exclaimed.

As Francesca and Natalia drove to a small wooden dock by the riverside, Natalia said, 'Francesca, the Environment Agency and I visited the factory this morning. The owners have fully admitted that they bought vast quantities of microbeads and when they were banned in all products, they were left with them. The cost to dispose of them legally was much higher than they had paid for them, so they were slowly, over time, putting them in the river.'

'What will happen to the owners?' Francesca asked.

'A huge monetary fine and public disapproval of all of their products. You have done a huge service for the public and the protection of the environment,' Natalia replied.

At the wooden dock, there was a small Environment Agency motor launch which had two men on it. Natalia had thought that Francesca would be keen to be part of the river clean up and the boat contained several extremely large nets, not the ones with holes in, but they were made of a light, solid material.

One of the men who was wearing a white, peaked hat stated in quite a high-pitched squeaky voice, 'I am the captain of this boat and you both must put on a life jacket. You must always be sitting down unless the boat is stationary. Am I quite clear?'

Natalia and Francesca started to giggle at each other about what the man was saying on such a small boat. Both nodded that they understood.

As they approached the white frothy mixture, Natalia and Francesca and the other man in the boat managed to scoop up as much of it as possible with the nets.

Over the last few days, the mixture had more or less stayed where Francesca had first seen it because there was very little wind or water movement.

Francesca hadn't dressed properly because each

time she pulled the net out of the water, she was getting increasingly wet. This was the third time that she had got wet because of these microbeads. She didn't care though, the fact that they were cleaning up the river was worth any discomfort she currently felt.

The captain of the boat was not helping with any of the clean-up operation and keeping out of the way of any water coming into the boat. At one stage, Francesca saw Natalia pretend to slip and splash the captain, which a little while later Francesca did the same. All of this was much to the annoyance of the captain but made both, Francesca and Natalia, laugh. Even his lovely white peaked hat was getting exceedingly wet!

When they had finished the clean-up and they had dried off with some towels that Natalia had brought, she took Francesca home. Francesca thought 'what a great team the two of them made' and when she grew up, they, as a team, would be able to, not only save the environment in Somersby but save the whole planet.

Chapter Seventeen

That Sunday afternoon, Francesca and Joseph went for a walk with their mum and dad. They walked to the Somersby ponds so that Francesca could show them where she had taken the pictures of the dragonflies and damselflies. She also showed them where the microbeads had been at the river pond edge. Francesca was pleased that it all looked clear now.

Then they walked around the ponds with Francesca showing her mum and dad the dragonflies and damselflies that were buzzing around.

Then they went along the main path through Somersby Woods. Joseph didn't point out where his den was, as he wanted to keep that a secret. He was pleased that there was no way you could make it out from the main path through the wood.

When they arrived home, Katherine and Alphonso finished off cooking the tasty summer BBQ that they had put together. The DeLuca family all sat around the garden table in pleasurable family company to eat their beefburgers and sausages together. They were happily chatting to each other, enjoying the food and the relaxing summer sun.

Alphonso asked, 'What has been the highlight of your week then, Joseph?'

He wanted to reply that it was making a den or finding the stolen property in a lock-up garage or being on a real, live police stakeout. He knew that Sergeant Price had told his parents all about what had happened, but instead he said, 'Scoring a penalty and winning a medal was fantastic, but also seeing Francesca slowly getting wet in the inflatable boat was probably my funniest moment this week.' Joseph quickly ducked out of the way of Francesca's arm as it shot out at him.

'What about you then Francesca?' her dad asked.

Francesca knew without a doubt that it was the discovery of who had put the microbeads into the river, but her parents knew all about that. So, she said, 'The funniest thing was Joseph getting off his cycle pretending that he had won some big cycle race (so she had seen him when he got home the other day then). However, I really enjoyed working with Natalia and imagining I was an environmental health officer.'

'So, what do you plan to do next week then?' their dad said.

Both of them replied almost in unison, 'Just chill out, Dad!'

Both Katherine and Alphonso knew that there was no way that this was going to happen with their two children. They were always immensely proud of Francesca and Joseph, but what they had done this week for the community had made them especially proud of their children and was incredible!

After they had all finished their meal, they settled themselves into comfy chairs in the garden to enjoy a relaxing time, reading books.

As soon as they had done this, the side gate to the garden banged open, and in marched Grandpa and Grandma DeLuca.

Grandma DeLuca came into the garden shouting loudly, 'Where are you, my *bambinos*? Grandma is here to see you!'

That was the end of any thoughts on having a relaxing and peaceful time, but Francesca and Joseph were delighted to see them both.

THE END

Author's Note

I made my first attempt at writing a fiction book in 2020. It was a DCI Alexander McFarlane crime mystery. My two eldest grandchildren, Jonah and Florence, asked me to write a story for them also, so here it is!

Somersby is an actual place; it is a little hamlet in the Lincolnshire Wolds, described exactly where it is geographically in this book. I picked Somersby because it is the birthplace of Alfred Lord Tennyson who was the Poet Laurette for most of the Victorian era. He has been in my younger days an inspiration to me.

Somersby is, of course, just a hamlet with only a handful of houses, so I used literary licence to create a fictional Somersby that exists in this story.

BV - #0040 - 040522 - C0 - 216/138/6 - PB - 9781803780177 - Gloss Lamination